The Bubbler

Created by: Thomas Astruc
Comics adaptation by: Nicole D'Andria
Written by: Thomas Astruc & Sébastien Thibaudeau
Art arranged by: Cheryl Black
English revision: Cindy Morrow
Lettered by Justin Birch

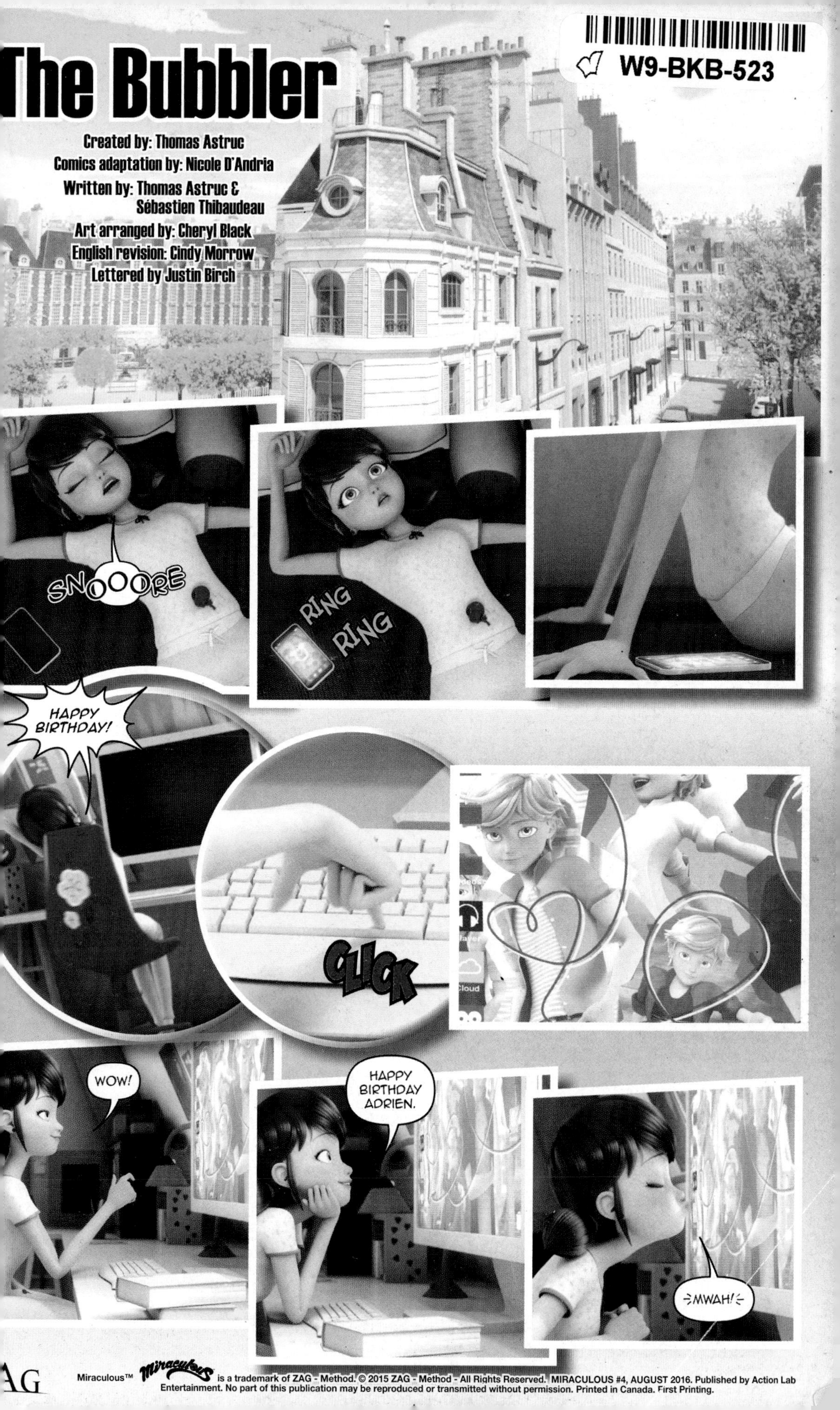

HAPPY BIRTHDAY ADRIEN!
OH PLAGG!

GET THAT FILTHY PIECE OF CAMEMBERT OUT OF MY FACE!
IF YOU INSIST!

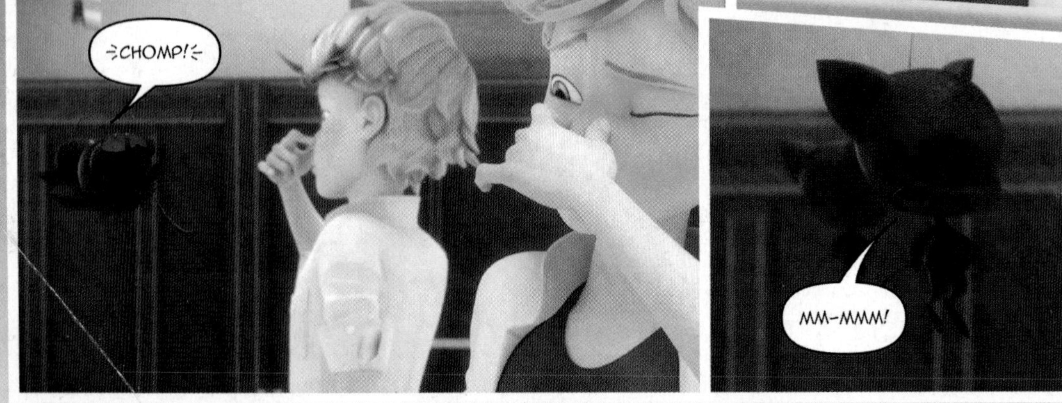
CHOMP!
MM-MMM!

I CAN'T DO IT! I CAN'T DO IT!

NO YOU DON'T GIRL! YOU'VE BEEN STALLING ALL MORNING. NOW'S THE TIME!

WAAAHH!

UH...

HEEE!
URH... HUHU... HEY...

...HEY?

WAIT! AM I SEEING WHAT I THINK I'M SEEING?
DON'T TELL ME IT'S ADRIEN'S BIRTHDAY!?!
GASP!

UH-HUH.
DO I HAVE TO DO EVERYTHING MYSELF?
SERIOUSLY, WHAT ARE YOU GOOD FOR?

I... UH...
...WANTED TO... UM, GIFT YOU A MAKE!
I MEAN, GIFT YOU A GIVE I MADE!
YAWN
I MEAN-
OUTTA THE WAY!
HAPPY BIRTHDAY, ADRIEN!
MWAH!
ER, YEAH. UH, THANKS CHLO'!

BRAT!
DID YOU GET THE GIFT I SENT YOU?
UH... NO?
WHAT?!
OH, THOSE DELIVERY GUYS!
I BET IT WAS TOO HEAVY SO THEY HAD TO GO BACK AND GET ANOTHER GUY TO HELP.
THOSE SLACKERS!
I'LL MAKE SURE THEY GET IT TO YOU BY TONIGHT!

SOUNDS LIKE YOU HAVE QUITE THE SURPRISE COMIN' YOUR WAY MAN!
YEAH, I GUESS...
GET BACK THERE! DON'T BE A PUSHOVER... LITERALLY!
WHAT DID YOU GET HIM?
I DIDN'T. YOU DID!
AND IT BETTER BE AMAZING, AND IT BETTER NOT BE LATE!!

ANYWAY, I WOULDN'T GIVE UP ON YOUR DAD JUST YET!
HONK HONK!
GOTTA GO. PHOTO SHOOT!
WHY CAN'T I JUST MEAN WHAT I SAY?
UH- SAY WHAT YOU MEAN?
EXACTLY!

HUUUH! THIS MAILBOX WON'T BUDGE!
RING THE DOORBELL.
ARE YOU KIDDING?! WHAT IF ADRIEN ANSWERS THE-
YES?
AH!
UHM... HI?

I'M IN ADRIEN'S CLASS AND I... UH... DID I ALREADY SAY THAT? UM...

GIGGLE.

UM...
...TEE-HEE.
PUT IT IN THE BOX.
THANK YOU!
SNAP!
OOOOHH, I HOPE HE LIKES IT!
YOU SIGNED THE NOTE, RIGHT?
NOOOOO!
GIRL, GIRL, GIRL...

WHO WAS THAT, NATHALIE?
A FRIEND OF ADRIEN'S. SHE WAS DELIVERING A GIFT FOR HIS BIRTHDAY.
BOOP
DID YOU REMEMBER TO BUY HIM A PRESENT FROM ME?
OF COURSE I DID!
GOOD.
ER, BUT YOU DIDN'T ASK ME TO!
YES, MR. AGRESTE. I- I'LL TAKE CARE OF IT!
BOOP
OH NO...

PHEW.
DING!
OH?
BOOP
YES?
UH... HI?
UM... THANKS FOR LETTING ME IN.
ADRIEN'S NOT HOME YET.
UH... I WAS COMING TO SEE YOU, DUDE- EEERH, SIR!
ME?

YEAH, THAT'S RIGHT. LOOK, I KNOW YOU DON'T WANT ADRIEN TO HAVE A PARTY, BUT-IT'S HIS BIRTHDAY, DUDE!
I- I MEAN SIR!
IT'S ALL HE WANTS-
NO. THAT'S FINAL.
NINO. YOU'RE HERE.
ANYTHING FOR MY BEST BUD!
SHOW SOME AWESOMENESS, DUDE! I MEAN SIR! PLEASE!

FORGET IT, NINO! REALLY. IT'S FINE.
LISTEN, YOUNG MAN. I DECIDE WHAT'S BEST FOR MY SON! IN FACT, I'VE JUST DECIDED YOU'RE A BAD INFLUENCE AND YOU'RE NOT WELCOME IN MY HOUSE EVER AGAIN! **LEAVE NOW!**
FATHER! NINO WAS JUST TRYING TO DO SOMETHING COOL FOR ME!
GOODBYE.

NINO WAIT!

I'M SORRY. MY FATHER, HE'S... PRETTY STUBBORN. IT JUST WORKS BEST TO STAY OUT OF HIS WAY.

IT'S NOT FAIR ADRIEN! HARSH!
UNCOOL!
THANKS ANYWAY, NINO.

SO UNCOOL...
BLOOP
BUT... DADDY!
PLLEEEASE!!!
NO! IT'S NOT PLAY TIME! YOU'VE GOT YOUR CHORES TO DO!
ARRH!
ADULTS RUIN EVERYTHING ALL THE TIME!

DESPERATE TO HELP HIS FRIEND BUT FEELING POWERLESS. HOW FRUSTRATING...
...IT WON'T BE LONG BEFORE FRUSTRATION TURNS TO ANGER!
WWZZING
FLY AWAY MY LITTLE AKUMA AND EVILIZE HIM!

BLOOP
BLOOP
FSSSH

HAWK MOTH IS MY NAME, AND BUBBLER IS NOW YOURS. I WILL HELP YOU WITH THESE HORRID ADULTS.
AND ALL YOU HAVE TO DO IN RETURN IS HELP ME GET SOMETHING FROM LADYBUG AND CAT NOIR...
YES, HAWK MOTH.
GURGLE
GURGLE

BURBLE BURBLE
NO MORE ADULTS MEANS TOTAL FREEDOM! THIS IS SOOOO SWEEEET!!
OFF THE HOOK!

WOOOSH
BURBLE
BURBLE
WHOA!

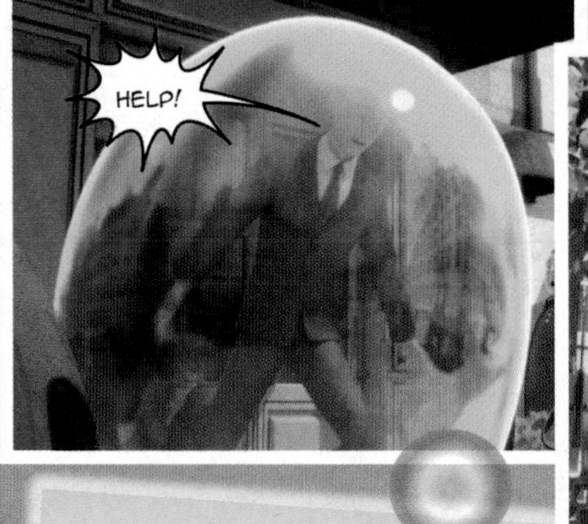
HELP!

WHAT?!

AAAH!

PERFECT!

MOM!
MOOOOM!
MARINETTE!
DAD?! DAAAD!
YOUR PARENTS!
HAWK MOTH MUST HAVE RELEASED ANOTHER AKUMA!
I'VE GOTTA FIND HIS NEWEST VILLAIN ASAP!

TIKKI! SPOTS ON!
TING
HA!
FWWSH
SWISH

AND NOW....
...PARTY TIME!!
WAAAH!
HEY HEY HEY! TODAY'S YOUR LUCKY DAY LITTLE DUDES!! THE ADULTS ARE TAKING THE DAY OFF! SO MAKE THE MOST OF IT!
NO CHORES, NO HOMEWORK, NO MORE NAGGING! JUST FUN FUN FUN! THIS IS THE BUBBLER'S GIFT TO YOU!
WAAAH!
OUVERT
TOUS LE
DON'T WORRY YOUR PARENTS WILL COME BACK! I'LL SEE TO IT!
YOU TAKE CARE OF THEM IN THE MEANTIME.

THE BUBBLER'S BROUGHT ALL YOUR HOMIES TOGETHER FOR ONE SINGLE SOLE PURPOSE-
-TO CE-LE-BRATE!
YAAAY!!!
COME ON NOW!
LET'S GET DIS PARTEH STARTED!!!
WRICKA-WRICKA!
COME ON EVERYBODY! I BROUGHT YOU HERE TO PARTY!
SO DANCE OR ELSE YOU'LL JOIN THE ADULTS UP IN THE SKY!
MWAAHAHAHAHA!
IT WON'T BE LONG BEFORE LADYBUG AND CAT NOIR SHOW UP TO MEET THEIR DOOM!
MWAAHAHAHAHA!

WHAT'S YOUR PROBLEM? RELAX! YOU'RE GETTING THE PARTY YOU ALWAYS WANTED!
BUT NINO'S BEEN AKUMATIZED! I'VE GOTTA HELP HIM!
YOU MAY NEVER GET THIS CHANCE AGAIN! COME ON, LET'S HAVE A LITTLE FUN WHILE YOUR FATHER'S AWAY!
THEN WE'LL SAVE NINO, TRAP HIS AKUMA, AND ALL'LL BE GOOD!
OK. YOU'RE RIGHT. THIS MIGHT BE THE FIRST DAY IN MY LIFE THAT I ACTUALLY GET TO DO WHAT I WANT FOR ONCE!

BOOM!
IT'S YOU AND ME, BUBBLER!

WOO-HOO!
HEY! NICE PARTY! I GUESS... SINCE IT'S MY FIRST ONE.
I'M REQUESTING A SLOW DANCE.
IT'S FOR ADRIEN.
HIS FIRST SLOW DANCE...
OOHHH!!! YOU KNOW IT GIRL!
IS IT ME OR DOES EVERYONE SEEM A BIT WEIRD?!

FORGET ABOUT THEM. LET'S GO DANCE! COME ON!
MMMH-
THERE IS NO WAY THIS IS HAPPENING!!!

LUCKY...
FWIP FWIP FWIP
...CHARM!
PHWOOSH!!
HUH?
A RECORD?

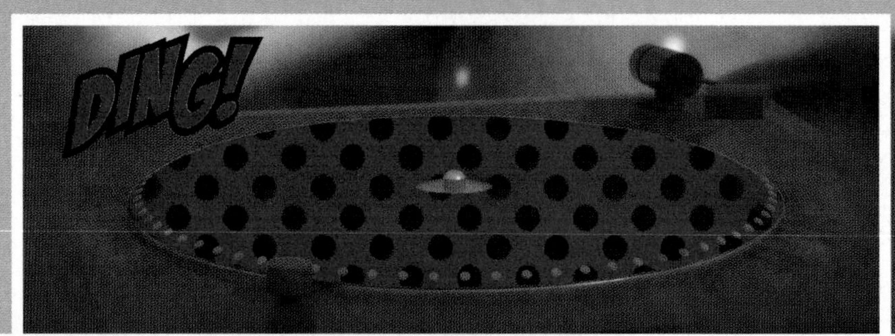
DING!

DING!

DING!

OK THEN...

...LET THE MUSIC PLAY!

WOOSH
CLACK!

HUH?
HEH HEH... GUESS WE'LL HAVE TO TAKE A RAIN CHECK ON THAT SLOW DANCE!
DUDE, WHO JUST HIJACKED MY MIX!?
YOURS TRULY!
BEEP BEEP!
HUH?
BETTER BUG OUT QUICK BEFORE I CHANGE BACK TO NORMAL!
SPOTS OFF!

FWWSH
SWOOSH
OOF!
MARINETTE...
IT WAS AN EMERGENCY!
YEAH, IF BY "EMERGENCY" YOU MEAN "JEALOUSY"! YOU KNOW WHAT HAPPENS ONCE YOU USE YOUR LUCKY CHARM! YOU ONLY HAVE MINUTES BEFORE-
-I TURN BACK. I KNOW. BUT I FIGURED, THE BUBBLER... HE'S NOT GOING ANYWHERE.
WE HAVE TIME TO GET YOU SOME FOOD TO GET YOUR ENERGY BACK UP!
THEN, WE'LL GET RIGHT BACK OUT THERE! I PROMISE...

I'VE GOTTA FIND A PLACE WHERE I CAN TRANSFORM– FAST!
WHERE HAVE YOU BEEN, GIRL!
I WAS SO SCARED SOMETHING HAD HAPPENED TO YOU!
ME TOO!
I'M SURE LADY BUG AND CAT NOIR WILL SHOW UP IN A MINUTE TO SAVE US ALL. THEY NEVER FAILED US! MEANWHILE, COME WITH ME! I HAVE GOT SOMETHING FOR YOU!
UH... THERE'S SOMETHING I HAVE TO DO FIRST!
IT'S ABOUT ADRIEN!
...OK.
MARINETTE! THE BUBBLER!
OK OK, IN A SEC!

LOOK!
NOW YOU CAN SIGN YOUR GIFT!
YES!

HEY, YOU! WHY AREN'T YOU HAVING FUN?!

NONE OF YOUR BUSINESS!

THEN I'M GONNA MAKE IT MY BUSINESS!

HAHA HAHA!

LOVE... MARINETTE!
SCRIBBLE SCRIBBLE
THERE!
MWAH!
PERFECT!
RIGHT! WE'RE GOOD! SPOTS ON, MARINETTE!
I CAN'T DO IT NOW!
ALYA'S HERE!
WHAT'JA SAY?
GO AHEAD! I'LL MEET YOU IN THE YARD!
PHEW.
OH NO!
YOU WERE RIGHT TIKKI, I NEVER SHOULD HAVE WAITED THIS LONG!

HEY, PARIS! HOW YA DOIN'?!
I CAN'T HEAR YOU!
UH... YAAAY?!
LADYBUG?

SORRY BUBBLER...

ZWOOP!

SWISH
...BUT THE PARTY'S OVER!
WHY YOU GOTTA BE LIKE THAT?
YOU MADE ALL THE ADULTS DISAPPEAR, THAT'S WHY!
AND NOW YOU'RE IMPRISONING ANYONE WHO ISN'T HAVING FUN...
ADRIEN?

YOU WILL NOT BUST UP MY PARTY!

BLOOP
BLOOP

WHIRR WHIRR
WHIRR WHIRR
POP!
YAAAAH!
AH!

I THINK I'VE BEEN A COMPLETE IDIOT!
PLAGG, CLAWS OUT!
TING
FWWSH

HEE-YAH!
HEH. THE LOOP THE LOOP'S NOT GONNA SAVE YOU!
FWWSH
FWIP
FWIP
BOING!
WHAT?!
FWOOP
LOOKS LIKE I MADE IT HERE JUST IN TIME!
I HAD IT UNDER CONTROL...
BOINK!
...BUT THANKS!

GET THEIR MIRACULUSES!
I WANT THOSE POWERS...
...NOW!!
TIME FOR A BUBBLE BATH!
BLOOP
BLOOP
BLOOP
POP
WHIRR WHIRR
WHIRR WHIRR
POP
POP
POP
POP
WHIRR WHIRR
POP
POP
WHIRR WHIRR
POP
I'LL PASS ON THE BUBBLES, THANKS.
AND THE BATH.

WELL, HOW WOULD YOU LIKE TO LIVE IN YOUR OWN LITTLE BUBBLE THEN?
BLOOP
BLOOP
BLOOP
BLOOP
SWISH
SWISH
SWISH
SWISH
SWISH
WHAT? THEY'RE STICKING TO ME!
SWISH
ME TOO!
SWISH
SWISH
SWISH
SWISH
SWISH
SWISH
SWISH
SWISH

MUAHAHAH!

WHOA...
BOP
BOP

GIVE ME YOUR MIRACULUSES BEFORE YOU RUN OUT OF AIR!
DREAM ON, BUBBLER!
TOTAL PARTY-POOPERS! JUST LIKE... ADULTS!
KIDS NEED ADULTS!
FALSE!
KIDS NEED FREEDOM! FUN! LET LOOSE AND LIVE IT UP! ADULTS ARE CONTROLLING AND BOSSY!

BUT ADULTS KEEP CHILDREN SAFE AND PROTECTED! THEY CARE FOR THEIR KIDS- THEY LOVE THEM!
MOST ADULTS DO, ANYHOW...
YOU MUST BRING THE ADULTS BACK!
NOPE! NEVER! KNOW WHAT? SINCE YOU CARE ABOUT THESE ADULTS SO MUCH...
...WHY DON'T YOU GO FLOAT WITH THEM FOR A WHILE!
GASP!
WHAM!
AAAAAAAAHHHHH!

AAAHHH!
WHAT DO YOU THINK YOU'RE DOING, BUBBLER?! YOU'RE SUPPOSED TO SEIZE THEIR MIRACULUSES!
FWUMP!
FWUMP!
USE YOUR CATACLYSM!
COULDN'T YOU HAVE SAID THAT 500 FEET AGO?!
WE CAN'T STAY STUCK IN THIS BUBBLE TOGETHER FOREVER!
SOUNDS PRETTY GOOD TO ME...
UGH!
CATACLYSM!
CRUNCH!
FWUMP!

POP
WHOA!
SHOULD WE SEE IF YOU LAND ON YOUR FEET THIS TIME?
NO THANKS!
YOUR STICK!
THERE!
GOT IT!
CLICK

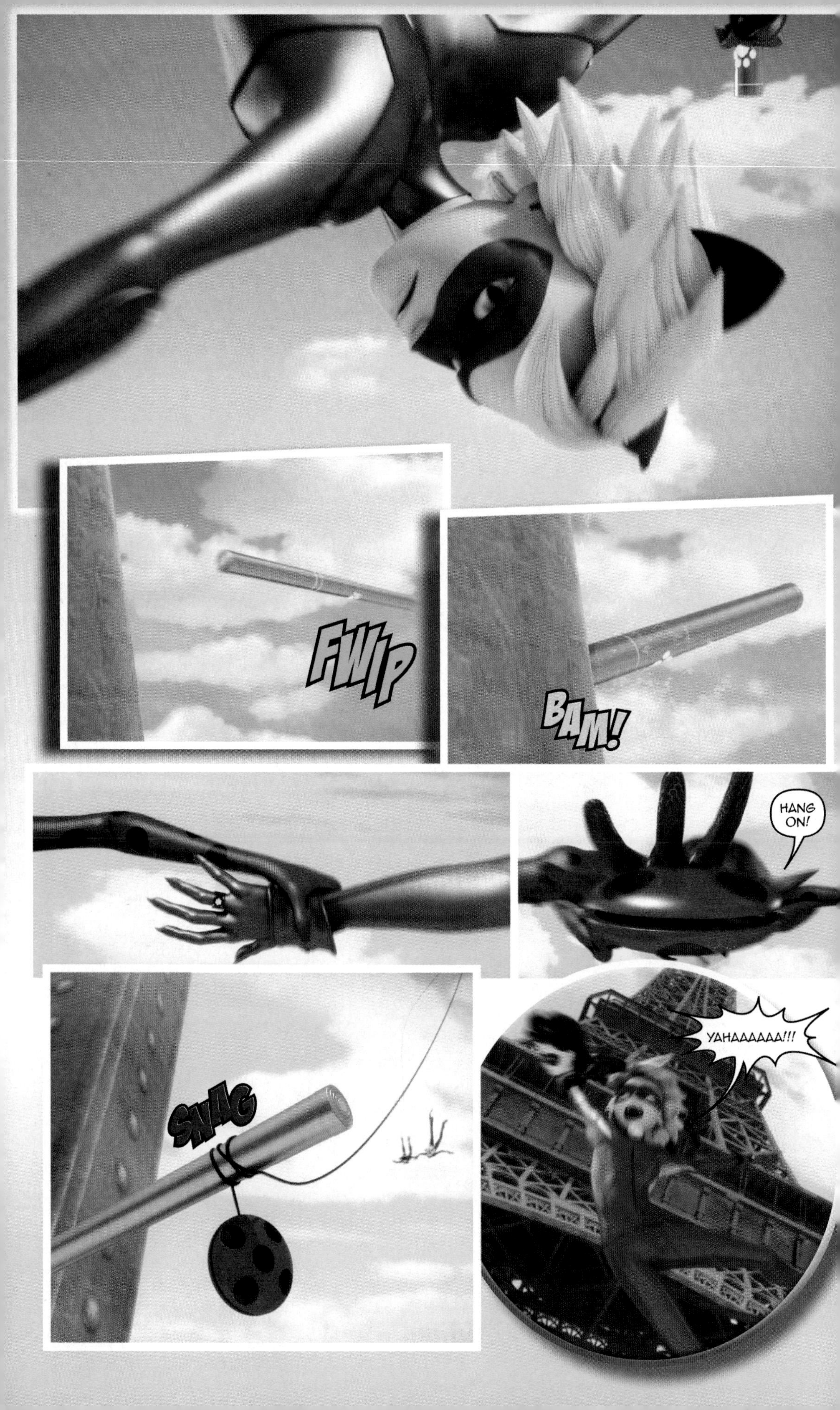
FWIP
BAM!
HANG ON!
SNAG
YAHAAAAAA!!!

GOOD THING CATS AREN'T AFRAID OF HEIGHTS!
WE'VE GOT TO GET TO HIS BUBBLE SWORD; THAT'S GOTTA BE WHERE THE AKUMA IS!
BEEP BEEP
BEEP BEEP BEEP
WE'D BETTER HURRY!

WHERE'S EVERYBODY? GET OUT HERE AND PARTY...
SORRY TO BURST YOUR BUBBLE.
LADYBUG!
LADYBUG!
LADYBUG!
LADYBUG!
NO ONE WANTS TO PARTY WITH YOU ANYMORE, BUBBLER!
WHAT'S WRONG WITH ALL YOU GUYS? WHY YOU ALL GOTTA BE SUCH HATERS?
GGGRRRRRRR!!!
BLOOP
BLOOP
BLOOP
BLOOP
NOOOO!

AAAH!
HELP!
OUTER SPACE IS THE NEXT STOP FOR YOUR PRECIOUS PEEPS!
AND THEY'RE NEVER COMING BACK!!!
STOP!
WHOOM!
SWISH!

SWOOSH
BLOOP
SWOOSH
BEEP
BEEP
BEEP
I'M GONNA SWITCH BACK SOON! HURRY!

LUCKY...
FWIP FWIP FWIP FWIP
...CHARM!
A... WRENCH?

BLOOP
BLOOP
HO...
...HYAH!
SWOOSH!

WHOA!
BOOSH!

YOUR AIM COULD USE A LITTLE WORK!
IS THAT ALL YOU GOT?!

WHAT TO DO WITH YOU...
HMM...
DING!
DING!
DING!

DING!
DING!
DING!

GOT IT!

CLINK

UGH!

HSSSSSS
CAT NOIR, COVER ME!

HSSSSSS
GOT IT!

HSSSSSS
GO ON!

YOU DUDES SERIOUSLY THINK THAT WILL STOP ME?!

BOING!
YAAA-
HMPH.
IT'S TIME TO BLOW YOU AWAY!
FHOOSH!
SNAG!
-AAAGH!
SNAP!
GET OUT OF HERE YOU NASTY BUG!

NO MORE EVIL DOING FOR YOU LITTLE AKUMA!
CLICK

TIME...

...TO DE-EVILIZE

SNAP!

GOTCHA!

SNAP!

BYE BYE LITTLE BUTTERFLY!

FWWSH
MIRACULOUS LADYBUG!

FWWSH

POP!
POP!

UGH...

HUH-WHA-DUDE?

POUND IT!

YOU CAN'T RUN FOREVER LADYBUG! AND WHEN I CATCH YOU I WILL CRUSH YOU!
I WILL DESTROY YOU BOTH!!!

BOOP
NATHALIE, DID MY SON LIKE HIS GIFT?
URH... ACTUALLY, UHM... I AM GOING TO CHECK RIGHT AWAY SIR!
GOOD.
BOOP
HMPH.
CRINKL
A BIRTHDAY PRESENT... FROM YOUR FATHER.
UH?! THANK YOU!
I MEAN... PLEASE SAY "THANK YOU" TO MY FATHER FOR ME.

WHAT DO YOU MEAN–
–NOT FOR A WEEK?!
THERE WERE NO ADULTS YESTERDAY TO DELIVER IT!
SO WHAT? RIDICULOUS! UTTERLY RIDICULOUS!!!
HA HA! SERVES CHLOÉ RIGHT!
HEY GIRLS!
HEY, THAT'S MY SCARF! HE'S WEARING MY SCARF!!
HEY DUDE!
YO, NICE SCARF ADRIEN! OFF THE CHAIN!

YEAH, CAN YOU BELIEVE MY DAD GOT THIS FOR ME? IT'S SO AWESOME! HE'S GIVEN ME THE SAME LAME PEN FOR THREE YEARS IN A ROW!
HUH?
WOW! I GUESS ANYONE CAN CHANGE! ADULTS CAN BE AWESOME WHEN YOU LEAST EXPECT IT!
SPEAKING OF ADULTS, I KNOW MY FATHER SAID YOU WERE A BAD INFLUENCE, BUT-
ADRIEN...
...WE'RE COOL! DON'T SWEAT IT. WE'RE BUDS, ALWAYS AND FOREVER.

YOU GOTTA TELL HIM *YOU'RE* THE ONE WHO KNITTED THE SCARF!
BUT HE SEEMS SO HAPPY ABOUT HIS DAD. I DON'T WANT TO SPOIL IT FOR HIM!
AWW, MARINETTE...
YOU'RE AMAZING, GIRL. YOU KNOW THAT, RIGHT? AND SOMEDAY ADRIEN WILL FIGURE IT OUT TOO... PROMISE.
THE END

Mr. Pigeon
Created by: Thomas Astruc
Comics adaptation by: Nicole D'Andria
Written by: Guillaume Mautalent & Sébastian Oursel
Art arranged by: Cheryl Black
Lettered by: Justin Birch
YOU'LL ONLY HAVE ONE DAY TO WORK ON YOUR FASHION PIECE.
DESIGN 18/05
AND IT MUST BE YOUR OWN DESIGN.
CONCOURS
IN 10 HOURS YOUR FINISHED PRESENTATION WILL BE JUDGED BY...
...NONE OTHER THAN THE GREAT FASHION DESIGNER, GABRIEL AGRESTE.
THE FATHER OF OUR VERY OWN STUDENT-
-ADRIEN AGRESTE!
DUDE!
IN FACT, ADRIEN WILL MODEL THE WINNING DESIGN IN HIS NEXT PHOTO SHOOT!

GASP

AND NOW TO ANNOUNCE THIS YEAR'S THEME.

DERBY HATS!

DERBY HATS???

YOU'VE GOT THIS GIRL!

YOU'RE.
GOING.
DOWN.

DERBY HAT? DERBY HAT?
DERBY HAT? DERBY HAT? I DON'T HAVE ANY DERBY HAT DESIGNS!
I'VE GOT TOP HATS...
...CAPS...
...EVEN TWO-HORNED HATS!
NEED A BERET?
I'M YOUR GIRL!
A SOMBRERO? NO PROBLEMO!
BUT A DERBY?!

FORGET IT, I'M A DISASTER ZONE. I'LL PROBABLY MESS EVERYTHING UP IN THE END...
WOW ALYA, THOSE ARE SOME AWESOME DESIGNS!
I DIDN'T KNOW YOU HAD SUCH MAD SKILLS.
THANKS ADRIEN, BUT I CAN'T TAKE THE CREDIT.
THESE SICK DESIGNS BELONG TO MARINETTE. OFF THE CHAIN, RIIIGHT?
HEE HEE.
YOU'RE SUPER TALENTED, MARINETTE!
R- REALLY?!
YOU SERIOUSLY HAVE A GOOD CHANCE OF WINNING.

WELL, UM, YEAH, I... LIKE... UM, DESIGNS THAT, UM... GO UPWARDS?
HUH?
UM, WHILE STOPPING?!
I MEAN, UH... UH... UGH... THANKS?
SURE... AND UH, GOOD LUCK!
MAYBE I'LL BE WEARING *YOUR* DERBY AT FATHER'S NEXT PHOTO SHOOT!
GIRL, YOU GOTTA GET A GRIP NEXT TIME! BUT DID YOU HEAR? ADRIEN THINKS YOU'RE GOOD ENOUGH TO WIN!
YAY!
HMPH!

DID YOU HEAR HOW IMPRESSED ADRIEN WAS WITH MARINETTE'S DE-
OF COURSE I HEARD! *HER?* WIN THE CONTEST? *AS IF!*
WHEN ADRIEN SEES *MY* DESIGN, HE'LL CONVINCE HIS FATHER TO AWARD *ME* THE WINNER!
I'M SURE HE WILL, CHLOE! YOU'RE A BORN CHAMPION! YOUR DESIGN WILL BLOW EVERYONE ELSE'S OUT OF THE WATER!
YEAH IT WILL... AS SOON AS I CAN GET MY HANDS ON THAT SKETCH PAD!
ONLY HAVE NINE HOURS UNTIL SHOW TIME!
YIKES!!!
I'M OFF TO MY "SECRET GARDEN" OF INSPIRATION! I'LL SEE YOU LATER!
SLAM!
UH-HUH... YOU GO GIRL.

THE TIME HAS COME FOR US TO FIND OUR NEXT VICTIM, MY WICKED LITTLE AKUMAS.
AND TO PREY UPON LADYBUG AND CAT NOIR.
THEIR MIRACULSES...
...MUST BE MINE!

SCRIBBLE
SCRIBBLE
SCRIBBLE
GEEZ, IT'S HARD TO BE CREATIVE UNDER PRESSURE...
MARINETTE, YOU SAVE THE WORLD UNDER PRESSURE!
I THINK DESIGNING A HAT SHOULD BE A PIECE OF CAKE.
HMM...
...A CAKE DERBY HAT. STYLISH **AND** TASTY! HA HA!

OH, THIS IS HOPELESS...
HUH?
RLOOO, RLOO!

WELL, HAPPY DAY! HAPPY DAY! SPLENDID IS THE AFTERNOON DAY!

COO!
COO!
COO!

AH, EDGAR, YOU FANCY ONE!

FANTASTIC! DAZZLING PERFORMANCE!

SCRAM, YOU WINGED RATS!

HOW MANY TIMES DO YOU NEED TO BE TOLD, MR. RAMIER?
POLICE

POLICE
POLICE
NO. FEEDING. THE PIGEONS!
IT'S STRICTLY FORBIDDEN. IF EVERYONE FEEDS THEM, THEY'LL LEAVE THEIR WASTE EVERYWHERE!

BUT... WHO'S GOING TO FEED MY POOR PIGEONS?
ALL THE PARK KEEPERS KNOW ABOUT YOU, MR. RAMIER! YOU'RE BANNED FROM EVERY PARK IN PARIS! LEAVE NOW, OR I'LL CALL THE AUTHORITIES!
POLICE
OH, WAIT... I'M THE AUTHORITY.
GET OUT!
SHEESH. I ALMOST FEEL SORRY FOR THAT MAN!
WHAT A UNIQUE CHARACTER! HE WAS LIKE... A HUMAN BIRD. ALL HE NEEDED WAS A FEATHER JACKET TO COMPLETE THE LOOK!
A FEATHER JACKET... HMM.
NICE THINKING, TIKKI!

MY POOR, POOR PIGEONS...
POOR MR. RAMIER. THE FEELING OF INJUSTICE...
...SUCH EASY PREY FOR MY AKUMA!
WWZZING
FLY AWAY MY LITTLE AKUMA AND EVILIZE HIM!

FSSSH
MR. PIGEON, I'M HAWK MOTH. NEITHER THIS POLICE OFFICER NOR ANY OTHER OF THE PARK KEEPERS SHOULD STOP YOU FROM TAKING CARE OF YOUR FRIENDS!
WHAT WOULD PARIS BE WITHOUT PIGEONS?! WHAT WOULD THE PIGEONS BE WITHOUT YOU?!
AHA!
GURGLE
GURGLE
GURGLE
GURGLE
RLOOO, RLOO!

SCRIBBLE SCRIBBLE
TIME TO GET MY DERBY DESIGN.
HM HM HMM...
YES!

SNAP!
PERFECT!
NOW THAT'S A DERBY!
THANKS TIKKI.
WE'RE SOOO AWESOME!
WE?

OH RIGHT, SORRY!
YOU'RE SOOO AWESOME, CHLOÉ!
WHEN ARE WE, UH, YOU GOING TO MAKE THE HAT?
OF COURSE NOT!
AND RUIN THESE NAILS?
DADDY'LL PAY SOMEONE TO DO IT!

YES!
OOF!
UH... SORRY MISTER OFFICER, SIR.
GIGGLE
HMPH.
WAAA!
FLUTTER
FLUTTER

COME ON! CAN WE GO ANY FASTER?
SORRY FOLKS. WE HAVE A SITUATION HERE; YOU'LL NEED TO GET OFF THE BUS NOW!
AAAH!
COO!
COO!
THIS IS... WEIRD.
PIGEONS HAVE TAKEN OVER PARIS!
RROOO ROLOOO !

THIS IS JUST ONE OF MANY ALARMING SITUATIONS GIVING AUTHORITIES CAUSE FOR MAJOR CONCERN!
NEWS
RROOO ROLOOO !

YES... I'VE JUST BEEN TOLD THAT SOMEONE NAMED "MR. PIGEON" IS MAKING AN ANNOUNCEMENT.
RROOO ROLOOO !

OH DREARY DAY, POOR PARISIANS!
RROOO ROLOOO !

RRRLOO RRRLOO!
ROOO ROLOOO !

SORRY TO RUFFLE YOUR FEATHERS, BUT PARIS NOW BELONGS TO THE PIGEONS!
RROOO ROLOOO !
RRRRLLOOO RRRRLOO!

I NEED TO TRANSFORM.

PARIS NEEDS US!
TIKKI, SPOTS ON!
TING
FWWSH
SWISH

NOW THIS IS WEIRDER THAN WEIRD!
BIRDS OF A FEATHER FLOCK TOGETHER!
ACHOOO!!!

I'M ALLERGIC TO FEATHERS.
CHOO!
THAT'S HELPFUL!
TELL ME ABOUT IT!
AA... AAA...
PHEW
THESE BIRDS ARE ONLY PART OF THE PROBLEM. THE PARK KEEPERS IN PARIS ARE VANISHING WITHOUT A TRACE!
WHA?

WE HAVE TO TRACK DOWN MR. PIGEON.
AND FAST!
WHERE WE GONNA FIND HIM?
SNIFFLE
HMMM... I DON'T KNOW WHERE WE CAN FIND HIM...
...BUT I DO KNOW WHERE HE CAN FIND US!

POLICE
ACT NATURAL, OR HE'LL NEVER SHOW UP!
WHAT D'YA MEAN? I AM ACTING "NATURAL"!
COO COO!
LADYBUG AND CAT NOIR! JOB WELL DONE BUDDY-BOYYY! PIGEONS WILL REIGN SUPREME!
POWER TO THE PIIIIGEONNNSSS! RROOO HOO HOO HOO!

WHERE IS HE? HE SHOULD HAVE BEEN HERE BY NOW!
WAAAA... CHOO!
AAAAH!
WHAT THE...?
CHOO! CHOO!
ACHOO!

ACHOO!
HUH?
WHERE'S THAT BIRD BRAIN MR. PIGEON?
HE'S GOTTA BE HERE SOMEWHERE!

IF YOU WANT TO GIVE PARIS BACK TO THE PIGEONS FOR GOOD, YOU MUST FIRST RID THE CITY OF THOSE TWO PESTS.
RLOO, RLOO!
CALL ME CRAZY, BUT I FEEL LIKE BIRDSEED ALL OF A SUDDEN!
GOT ANY BRIGHT IDEAS, BUG?
YOU'RE THE CAT! DON'T YOU EAT THESE THINGS FOR BREAKFAST?
LOOK!

WE'RE TRAPPED!

ROOHOO! ROOHOO! CHIRPY DAY!

I'M SO RUTHLESS!

EXCELLENT! NOW... TAKE THEIR MIRACULUS!

RLOOO, RLOOO! YOUR MIRACULUS—GIVE THEM TO ME! OR FACE THE WRATH OF MY FEATHERED FRIENDS!

RROOO ROOLOOO!

BAM!
BAM!
BAM!

WHAT ARE THEY DOING?!
CHOO!
BAM!
BAM!
BAM!
YOU'VE GOT TO BE KIDDING ME...
NO JOKES HERE. MY FEATHERED FRIENDS ARE PREPARED TO DO WHATEVER IT TAKES!
DA DA DEEE, ON THE COUNT OF THREE, MY BELOVED PIGEONS WILL COMMENCE FIRE!
YOU CAN STILL SAVE YOUR SORRY SKINS BY HANDING ME YOUR MIRACULUS.
ONE...
...TWO...
CAT NOIR, THE BARS!

I'M ON IT!
CRUNCH!
CATACLYSM!

SCREEEKK!
WHAT?!

WELL, WELL. LOOKS LIKE THE PIGEON'S REALLY A CHICKEN!
RROOO ROOLOOO!
MEEE??? I'M NOT FLYING AWAY!
I'M JUST KILLING TWO BIRDS...

...WITH ONE STONE!
RROOO ROOLOOO!
RLOOOOO!
HUH?
OH NO...
ROOHOOHOOHOO!
ONWARD MY BEAUTIFUL BIRDS OF PREY!

SLAM!
I'M NOT DONE WITH YOU YET!
BANG!
ROOHOOHOOHOO!

BEEP
BEEP
I GOTTA GET OUTTA HERE BEFORE MY SECRET IDENTITY IS REVEALED.
YEAH... YOU WOULDN'T WANT TO LET THE CAT OUT OF THE BAG!
HA HA, VERY FUNNY!
LADYBUG, CAT NOIR! I'M IN GREAT DANGER...
...OF LOSING BIG BUCKS IF MY GUESTS LEAVE PARIS! YOU ARE GOING TO GET RID OF THOSE PIGEONS, AREN'T YOU?
OF COURSE WE ARE!
BUT BEFORE WE DO, I... HAVE AN URGENT NEED!
AN URGENT NEED?!
I SEE... HEAD TO THE ROYAL SUITE!

THERE'S PAPER IN THERE, BUT PERHAPS YOU'D PREFER... A LITTER TRAY?
UH? OH, RIGHT. NO LITTER TRAY NECESSARY! BUT UM, COULD I ALSO HAVE SOME CAMEMBERT BROUGHT UP?
THANKS!
'SCUSE-ME-SORRY-EMERGENCY!
KNOCK
KNOCK
KNOCK

HOW DO YOU LIKE YOUR CAMEMBERT?
RUNNY!
KNOCK KNOCK KNOCK
UNPASTEURIZED SAINT-CLAQUEAUCE, MATURED FOR TWO YEARS.
THANKS!
PHEW
BE-BLOOP
CHOW DOWN BUDDY, LADYBUG'S GOING TO NEED OUR HELP!
WHOA HO!

GREAT, I CAN GET A MUCH BETTER VIEW FROM UP HERE!
ODD... THEY'RE ALL FLYING IN THE SAME DIRECTION...
BETTER GO FOLLOW THEM!
READY WHEN YOU ARE, M'LADY.
LET'S GO!

SO THAT'S WHERE MR. PIGEON'S KEEPING THE PARK KEEPERS HE ABDUCTED!

THE GRAND PALAIS.

AAAAA... AAAAA...

MY PIGEON RADAR IS ON HIGH ALERT. LET'S SET THE CAT AMONG THE PIGEONS!
HOLD UP, KITTY! IT'S... TOO EASY.
I'VE GOT A PLAN!
PERFECT TIMING, HOE DEE HOE! WE'RE READY TO GREET THEM, AREN'T WE? THEY'RE GOING TO FALL RIGHT INTO MY TRAP!
IT WON'T BE LONG BEFORE YOU GET YOUR MIRACULUS, FRIEND.
I CAN'T WAIT, MY DEAR PIGEON.
IF WE CAN DESTROY THAT BIRD CALL, WE'LL BE ABLE TO CAPTURE THE AKUMA!
OK, YOU OPEN THE WINDOW.

I'LL GRAB HIM AND YANK HIM UP ON TO THE ROOF.
THEN YOU SNAG HIS BIRD CALL AWAY FROM HIM.
LET'S GO. EARLY BIRD GETS THE WORM!
AAA... AAA...
WHIR
WHIR WHIR
WAAACHOOO!!!
AAAH!

?
FWOOSH
CLANG!
CLACK!
SO MUCH FOR THE ELEMENT OF SURPRISE.

YOU'VE CAUGHT US ON A "FOWL" DAY!
RROOO, RROOO!
WE CAN'T LET HIM GET AWAY AGAIN!
STOP!
RLOOO, RLOO!

COO
COO
COO
COO
COO
COO
COO
COO
COO
DIDDITY DEE DEE!
COME CLOSER, I HAVE A BONE TO "PECK" WITH YOU!
I'D BE HONORED.
HE'S COMING IN FA-

CAT NOIR!
WHOA!
OOF...
POW!
AAAH!
GET US OUTTA HERE, LADYBUG!

LUCKY...
FWIP FWIP FWIP
...CHARM!
A COIN?! WHAT AM I SUPPOSED TO DO WITH THIS?

WHAT ELSE CAN I USE...?
DING!
DING!
DING!
DING!
DING!

YOU CAN'T "BUY" YOURSELF OUT OF THIS.
WHIR
WHIR
WHIR
WHIR
SNAG!

DON'T BET ON THAT!
IT'S FEEDING TIME FOR YOUR LITTLE FRIENDS...
CLINK

CLICK
RUMBLE RUMBLE
CAT NOIR!
HIT IT!

SNACK TIME!
POP
COO
COO
POPCORN?
OH NO...
STOP!!!

TIME TO FLY, BIRD BRAIN!
SKREEE
MY BIRD CALL! NOOOO!!!
CAT NOIR, GRAB IT!
NO PROBLEM LB! I'VE GOT-

ACHOO!!!
NO!
HURRY, WE NEED TO DESTROY IT!
RROOO!
OOPS.
NO YOU DON'T! IT'S MINE!
CLACK!

HYAAAA!
AAAAAH!
RROOOO!

LET GO!
WE'RE DOING THIS FOR YOUR OWN GOOD!
SMASH!
YES!
OW, MY HAND!
GASP

NO MORE EVIL DOING FOR YOU LITTLE AKUMA!
TIME TO DE-EVILIZE!
SNAP!
GOTCHA!
CLICK

BYE BYE LITTLE BUTTERFLY!
MIRACULOUS...
...LADYBUG!
FWWSH
FWWSH

FWWSH
WHUZZAT?

WHAT APPENED? HERE AM I?
POUND IT!

WRETCHED PIGEONS.
WRETCHED LADYBUG.
I'LL DESTROY EVERY ONE OF YOU!

THERE'S NO TIME TO LOSE! I HAVE LESS THAN AN HOUR!
00:58:22
VRRRRR
VRRRRR
00:34:00
ALMOST DONE! JUST... ONE MORE... THING...
00:03:41

Marinette +33653257
RING!
RING!
RING!
RING!
WHERE IS THAT GIRL?!
HELLO, MR. DAMOCLES. I AM MR. AGRESTE'S EXECUTIVE ASSISTANT, NATHALIE.
HELLO MISS! PARDON ME, BUT UH, WHERE IS MR. AGRESTE?
I'M HERE.
AH! URH... HELLO MR. AGRESTE. WELCOME TO OUR SCHOOL!

OH, THERE'S MR. AGRESTE! HE'S COMING THIS WAY!

WHERE HAVE YOU BEEN? YOU GOT YOUR HAT?

HUFF
YEP.
HUFF

HERE!

WELL, WHAT DO YOU THINK?
IT'S...

...THE SAME AS CHLOE'S!
WHAT?!

HI MR. AGRESTE! I'M CHLOE BOURGEOIS. YOU KNOW MY FATHER, ANDRÉ BOURGEOIS, THE MAYOR?
OOOH! THAT THIEVING LITTLE BRAT!
D'YOU WANT ME TO TAKE CARE OF IT?
I THINK I CAN HANDLE THIS.
HMM...
...TURN THE TABLET BACK TO MISS. BOURGEOIS' HAT!
IS THIS A JOKE?

NO FAIR! MARINETTE COPIED MY DESIGN! IT'S SCANDALOUS!
HOW COULD YOU DO THAT?
BOO HOO HOO HOO!
I APOLOGIZE FOR THIS SITUATION, MR. AGRESTE.
BUT I CAN PROVE THAT THIS DERBY HAT IS MY ORIGINAL DESIGN.
GO AHEAD.
UMM... EVERYTHING ON MY DERBY HAT IS HANDMADE, FROM THE EMBROIDERY TO THE WEAVING OF THE BAND TO THE STITCHING OF THE BRIM, ALL DONE BY MYSELF.
AND LAST, THERE'S A SPECIAL DESIGN ELEMENT THAT ONLY THE TRUE DESIGNER KNOWS ABOUT.
I SIGNED IT.

VERY EXQUISITE CREATION. YOU DEFINITELY HAVE THE LABORING HANDS OF A HAT MAKER, MISS...
...MARINETTE.
CONGRATULATIONS N YOUR DEMONSTRATION, MISS MARINETTE. YOU'RE THE WINNER.
THANK YOU!
ADRIEN VILL WEAR YOUR DERBY ON OUR EXT ADVERTISING CAMPAIGN.
OH!
AWESOME JOB, MARINETTE!

HEE. YOU'RE AWESOME... I MEAN, THANK YOU!

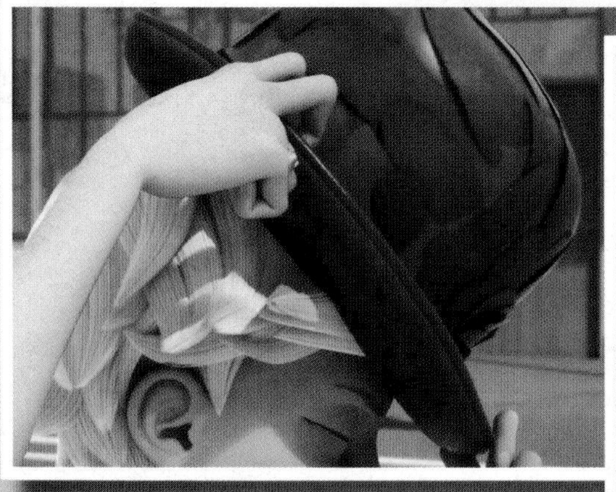

AAA...

WACHOO!!!

SORRY, I'M ALLERGIC TO FEATHERS.

GESUNDHEIT!

WOOHOO!
THE END.

Rogercop
reated by: Thomas Astruc
omics adaptation by: Nicole D'Andria
Vritten by: Denis Bardiau
rt arranged by: Cheryl Black
ettered by: James M. Birch
READY PAPA?
AS MUCH AS I'LL EVER BE.
HAPPY CAREER DAY, MY DARLINGS!
MY DAY EGINS AT 4 A.M. VERY MORNING, BECAUSE THE AKERY OPENS AT 7.
REC

YOU'D THINK THE LIFE OF A BAKER IS PRETTY ROUTINE, MAKING THE SAME PASTRIES, ROLLS, CAKES... BUT ACTUALLY, IT'S DIFFERENT EVERY DAY!
ONE DAY SOMEONE MIGHT ORDER A CAKE IN THE SHAPE OF THE EIFFEL TOWER.
AND ANOTHER DAY YOU MIGHT HAVE TO BAKE A THOUSAND-
YOU'VE REACHED THE VOICEMAIL OF GABRIEL AGRESTE'S OFFICE. PLEASE LEAVE A MESSAGE.
HI FATHER, IT'S ME. IT'S PARENTS' CAREER DAY AT SCHOOL, REMEMBER?
I WAS HOPING THAT YOU WERE GONNA SHOW UP... CALL ME BACK?
CLICK
-SIGH-
YOU OKAY?
YEAH, WHATEVER. NOTHING NEW...
CLAP
CLAP
CLAP
CLAP
HE'S NOT COMING IS HE? SORRY DUDE.

MARINETTE WILL COME AROUND AND PASS OUT SOME CROISSANTS BAKED FRESH THIS MORNING!
THANK YOU, MR. DUPAIN. NOW, LET'S MEET ALYA'S MOM.
SHE IS THE HEAD CHEF AT THE GRAND PARIS HOTEL, OWNED BY OUR MAYOR, MR. BOURGEOIS.
OH...
OH WOW!
IT'S BEAUTIFUL!
LOOK, DON'T TOUCH!
PUT IT AWAY, CHLOÉ! IT COULD GET IN THE WRONG HANDS...

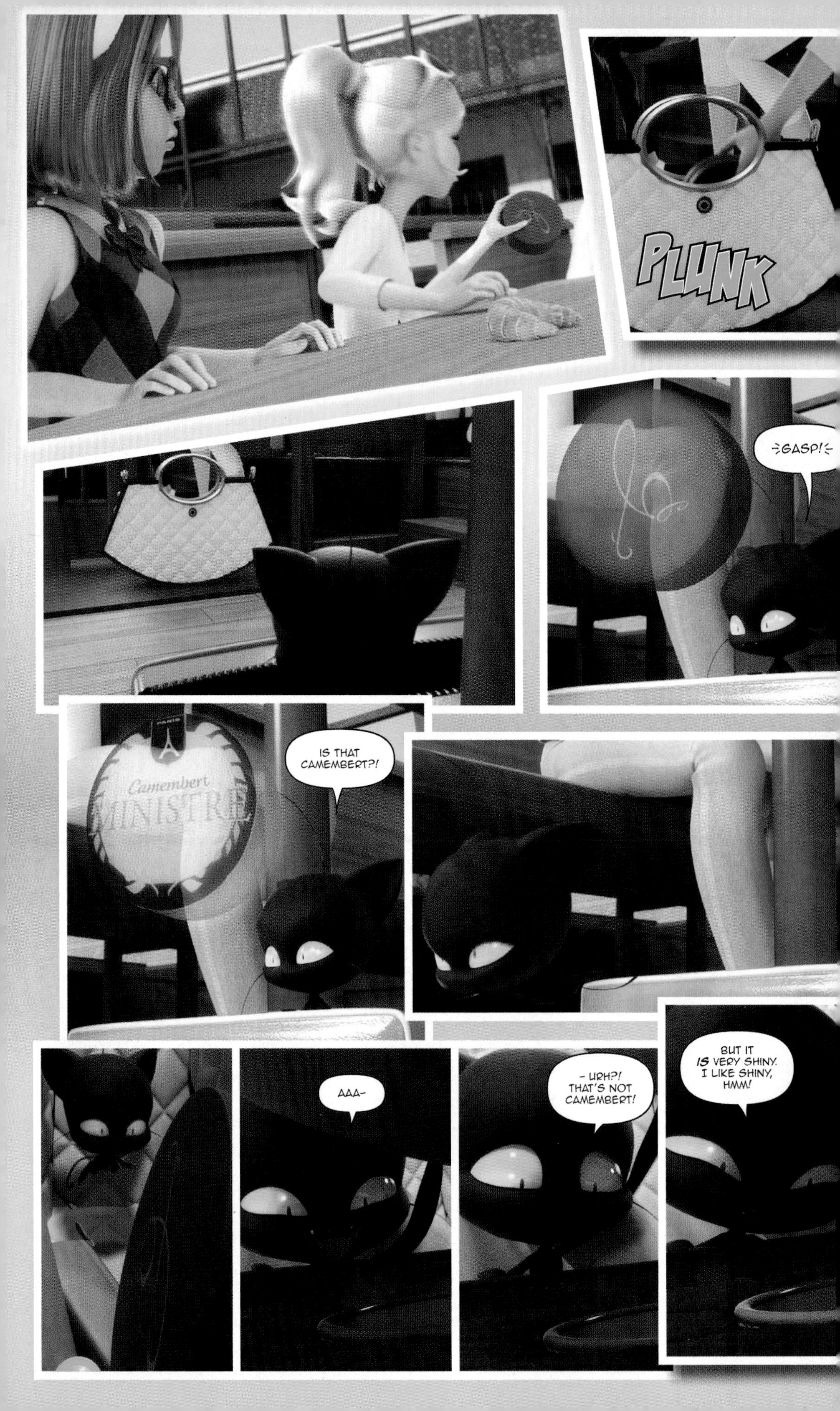
PLUNK
GASP!
IS THAT CAMEMBERT?!
Camembert MINISTRE
AAA-
- URH?! THAT'S NOT CAMEMBERT!
BUT IT *IS* VERY SHINY. I LIKE SHINY, HMM!

Histoire
WAAH!
GEEZ!
UGH...
IS THERE A DAY WHEN YOU'RE **NOT** TRIPPING OVER SOMETHING?

NEXT ON THE LIST IS SABRINA'S FATHER, A POLICEMAN. OFFICER ROGER!
URG... OOF...

POLICE
I'VE BEEN A POLICE OFFICER FOR 15 YEARS, AND I FIRMLY BELIEVE THAT EVERY CITIZEN IS INNOCENT UNTIL PROVEN GUILTY!

MY BRACELET! IT'S GONE!!

I HAD IT A SECOND AGO.

YOU! YOU STOLE IT!

WHAT? WHAT ARE YOU TALKING ABOUT?!

YOU PURPOSEFULLY TRIPPED ON MY BAG SO YOU COULD STEAL MY BRACELET!

MY DAUGHTER IS **NOT** A THIEF!

TWEEEET

HOLD ON A MINUTE, MISS. BOURGEOIS. WE DON'T ACCUSE WITHOUT PROOF.

MAYBE YOU SIMPLY MISPLACED YOUR BRACELET?

WHA-?!
YOU'RE CALLING *ME* A LIAR?
DADDY!
I- UH...
ROGER! I DEMAND YOU SEARCH THIS GIRL!
IMMEDIATELY.
HA!
ROGER? WHY ARE YOU JUST STANDING THERE? NEED I REMIND YOU THAT, AS MAYOR OF THIS CITY, *I* AM YOUR SUPERIOR?!

BUT SIR, IT'S AGAINST THE LAW! I CAN'T JUST GO-
POLICE
ALRIGHT, THEN YOU'RE NO LONGER A POLICE OFFICER!
MAYOR, YOU CAN'T BE SERIOUS?!? OVER A MISSING BRACELET?!
THIS IS MY DAUGHTER'S BRACELET WE ARE TALKING ABOUT! YOU'RE INCOMPETENT, AND YOU'RE FIRED!
GET OUT!!!
POLICE
GOOD! LET'S CALL LADYBUG! I'M SURE SHE'LL ACTUALLY DO SOMETHING...

PARENT-CHILD RELATIONSHIPS CAN BE SO COMPLICATED...
...AND A PERFECT BREEDING GROUND FOR STRESS.
WHEN THERE'S NO MORE LAW AND ORDER, THERE'S ONLY CHAOS LEFT.
WWZZING
FLY AWAY MY EVIL LITTLE AKUMA, AND TAKE CONTROL OF THIS POLICEMAN...

HE EXPECTS ME TO BREAK THE LAW? THAT'S JUST... JUST...
...CRIMINAL!
FWWSH
ROGERCOP, I AM HAWK MOTH. THIS CITY NEEDS A TRUE, RUTHLESS RIGHTER OF WRONGS! AND THAT IS WHERE YOU COME IN.

YES, SIR!
GURGLE GURGLE
YOU WILL SEIZE LADYBUG AND CAT NOIR'S MIRACULOUSES FOR ME. DO WE HAVE AN AGREEMENT?
LADYBUG AND CAT NOIR MUST BE DESTROYED IF YOU WANT TO ATTAIN ULTIMATE RETRIBUTION!
AFFIRMATIVE. CAT NOIR AND LADYBUG WILL BE POWERLESS AGAINST ME, AND JUSTICE WILL PREVAIL IN THE STREETS OF PARIS!

DON'T EVEN THINK OF GETTING NEAR MY DAUGHTER OR HER BAG!
DO YOU KNOW WHO I AM?!
PLEASE, GENTLEMEN. THIS IS A SCHOOL HERE... THINK OF THE CHILDREN! SURELY THE BRACELET IS AROUND HERE SOMEPLACE!
IT PROBABLY JUST...
...ROLLED OUT OF HER BAG OR SOMETHING!
IF I WERE HER BRACELET, I'D TRY AND GET AS FAR AWAY AS POSSIBLE FROM THAT CRAZY BRAT, TOO!
GIGGLE
HEY!
NINO'S BEEN FILMING THIS WHOLE TIME!

TOSS
HMPH!
THOOM
YOU'RE UNDER ARREST.

WHAT? WHAT FOR?!
YOU THREW LITTER ON A PUBLIC SIDEWALK, JAYWALKED AND CROSSED DURING A RED LIGHT...
WELL, I SUPPOSE I DID... BUT YOU CAN'T JUST **ARREST** ME!
WHO ARE YOU, ANYWAY? YOU DON'T LOOK LIKE A POLICEMAN!
PSSSHHEW
I SENTENCE YOU TO TRASH DUTY!

TWEET
AH!
OOF!
WHY-
CAN'T I-
STOP?!
NEXT MISSION:
SEEKING JUSTICE
FROM MAYOR
BOURGEOIS!

GIVE ME THE TAPE! I'LL HAVE IT ANALYZED BY PROFESSIONALS...
NO WAY! IT'S MY CAMERA!
WHO DO YOU THINK YOU'RE DEALING WITH? I AM THE MAYOR OF THIS CITY!
URK! GURK!
OOF!
HUH?!
WHERE'S THE SCHOOL PRINCIPAL? I WANT TO SEE THE PRINCIPAL!

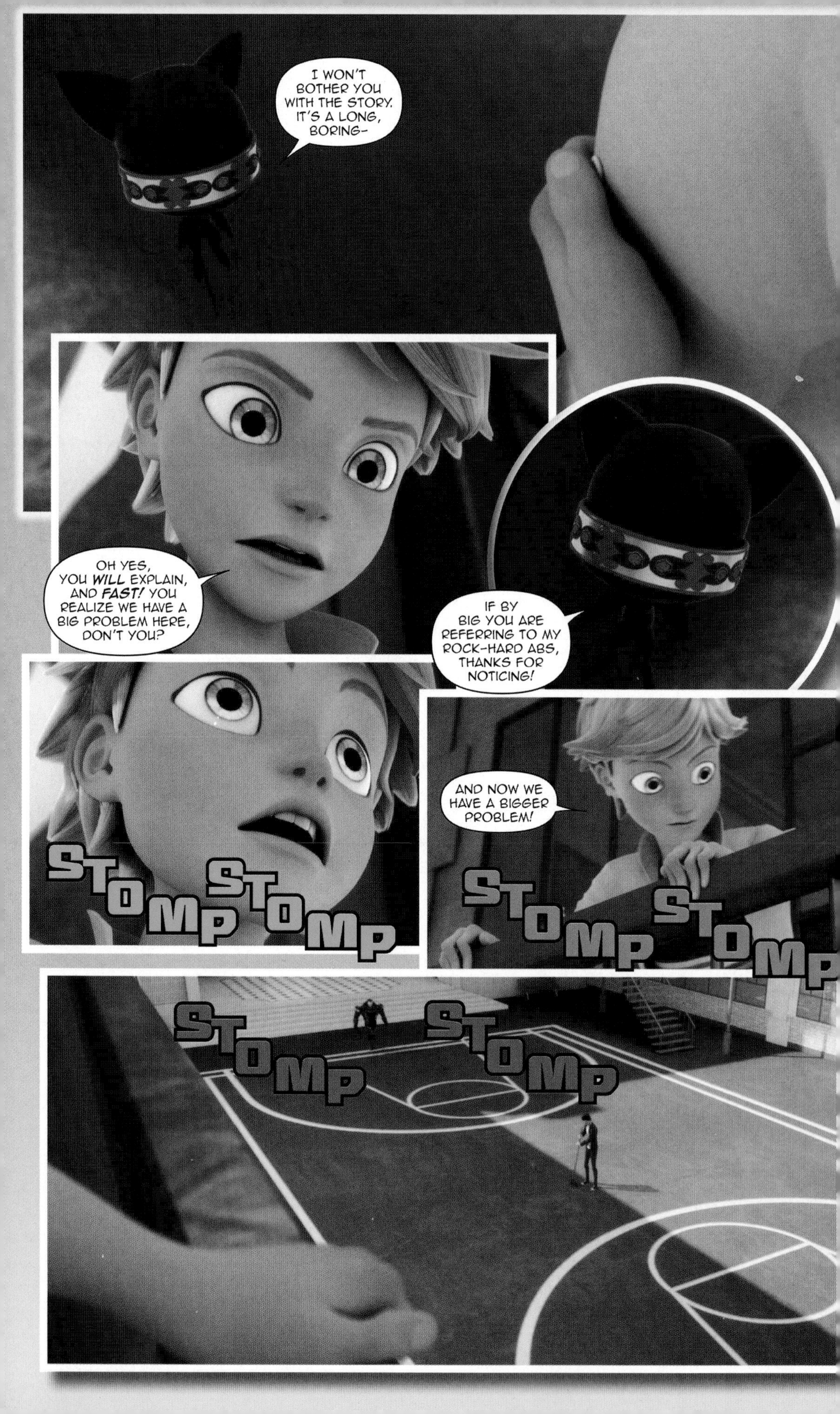
I WON'T BOTHER YOU WITH THE STORY. IT'S A LONG, BORING-
OH YES, YOU *WILL* EXPLAIN, AND *FAST!* YOU REALIZE WE HAVE A BIG PROBLEM HERE, DON'T YOU?
IF BY BIG YOU ARE REFERRING TO MY ROCK-HARD ABS, THANKS FOR NOTICING!
STOMP STOMP
AND NOW WE HAVE A BIGGER PROBLEM!
STOMP STOMP
STOMP STOMP

HEY, YOU CAN'T JUST WALK IN HERE!
I CAN GO WHEREVER I WANT, WHENEVER I WANT. I *AM* THE LAW!
W-WELL, *I'M* THE AUTHORITY AROUND HERE!
WHAT?!
YOU ARE GUILTY OF OBSTRUCTING THE PATH OF JUSTICE. I SENTENCE YOU TO MOVE AROUND.
TWEET
I CAN'T CONTROL MY ARMS! WHAT ARE YOU-
WHAT DO YOU MEAN I CAN'T TRANSFORM?!
IF YOU TRANSFORM, THE BRACELET WILL GET ABSORBED WITH ME AND DAMAGE YOUR POWERS!
MWAHAHAHAHA!
IT WON'T BE LONG BEFORE LADYBUG AND CAT NOIR SHOW UP TO MEET THEIR DOOM!

DAD?!
THAT'S HER DAD?!
UH, HELLO. MAY I HELP YOU?
WHERE IS THE MAYOR?
I THINK HE ALREADY LEFT, SIR...
ARE YOU LYING?
YES- I MEAN, NO!
IF NOBODY SPEAKS UP, I'LL PUT YOU ALL UNDER ARREST!
WHERE IS YOUR FATHER?!
I DON'T KNOW!

HM?
MR. PRINCIPAL, I DEMAND THAT YOU FIND WHO STOLE MY DAUGHTER'S BRACELET ASAP! OR YOUR JOB IS ON THE LINE, SIR!
BUT MR. MAYOR, I DON'T-
IT'S AN EXTREMELY VALUABLE PIECE OF JEWELRY!
STOMP STOMP
I WAS ONLY TRYING TO DEFEND MYSELF.
BUT MY DAD'S RIGHT; I ENDED UP ACCUSING EVERYONE IN THE PROCESS!
TRUTH IS, TIKKI, I DON'T THINK ANY OF US TOOK IT!
I'M SURE YOU'LL FIND A WAY TO MAKE IT RIGHT...
YEAH, WELL, RIGHT NOW, I'VE GOT TO TRANSFORM.

TIKKI, SPOTS ON!
TING
FWWSH

AAA-!
URGH...
AAAH!
AAAH!
I THOUGHT IT WAS A CAMEMBERT BOX!
ANYONE CAN MAKE A MISTAKE!
YOU'RE ALWAYS THINKING WITH YOUR STOMACH!
WAIT, THAT'S IT!
A BIT OF PEPPER...
SHAKE
SHAKE

SNIFF SNIFF
ACHOO!
POP!

GESUNDHEIT!

PLAGG, CLAWS OUT!
FWWSH
TING

SLAM!
I'M WARNING YOU: IF YOU DON'T FIND MY DAUGHTER'S BRACELET BY THIS EVENING, I'LL CUT OFF ALL YOUR CITY FUNDS FOR THE SCHOOL.
UNDERSTOOD?!
BUT SIR, HOW AM I SUPPOSED TO-
BAM!
DIDN'T ANYONE EVER TEACH YOU TO KNOCK BEFORE YOU COME IN?!

JUSTICE DOESN'T NEED AN INVITATION. MAYOR, YOU ARE UNDER ARREST FOR ABUSE OF POWER!
HA! LOOK WHO'S TALKING!
SNAG!
FWIP
HRRRPH!
LADYBUG! PARIS HAS A NEW RIGHTER OF WRONGS!
PEW
YOUR SERVICES ARE NO LONGER REQUIRED.
WHOA!
RRR...
I CAN'T LET YOU GO AROUND ACCUSING EVERYONE OF EVERY LITTLE WRONGDOING!

PEW
PEW
PEW

MR. ROGERCOP, I NEED YOUR HELP!
BEEP
BEEP
BEEP
AAGH!
UM, HELLOOO?!
HEY! COME BACK!
THOOM

SNAG!
HUFF
YAAAH!
OOH...

PEW
AH!
PATISSERIE
PATISSERIE
SLAM!
VROOM
YOU ARE OBSTRUCTING JUSTICE, CAT NOIR.

YOU ARE GOING TO PAY FOR THIS!
YOU CAN ADD "BODILY HARM" TO THE CHARGES!
PEW
PEW
YAAGH!
WHOA!
UGH...
LISTEN!

YOU'RE SABRINA'S DAD AND A GOOD COP. DON'T LET THE EVIL PERSON WHO GAVE YOU THESE POWERS MAKE AN EVIL COP OUT OF YOU!
I...
DON'T LISTEN TO THAT LIAR! TAKE THEIR MIRACULOUSES! THEIR POWERS BELONG TO ME!!!
JUSTICE **MUST** PREVAIL IN THE STREETS OF PARIS!

PEW
PEW
PEW
AAAAAH!
THE MAYOR MUST PAY FOR GETTING RID OF HIS BEST POLICE OFFICER!

MR. ROGERCOP!
I'VE GOT A SERIOUS PROBLEM, WORSE THAN A BAD HAIR DAY!
COME WITH ME AND WE'LL TALK ABOUT IT.
CHLOÉ, NO!
THUMP!

HUH?!
A FLYING CAR? SERIOUSLY!?!
I BET YOU MISSED ME!

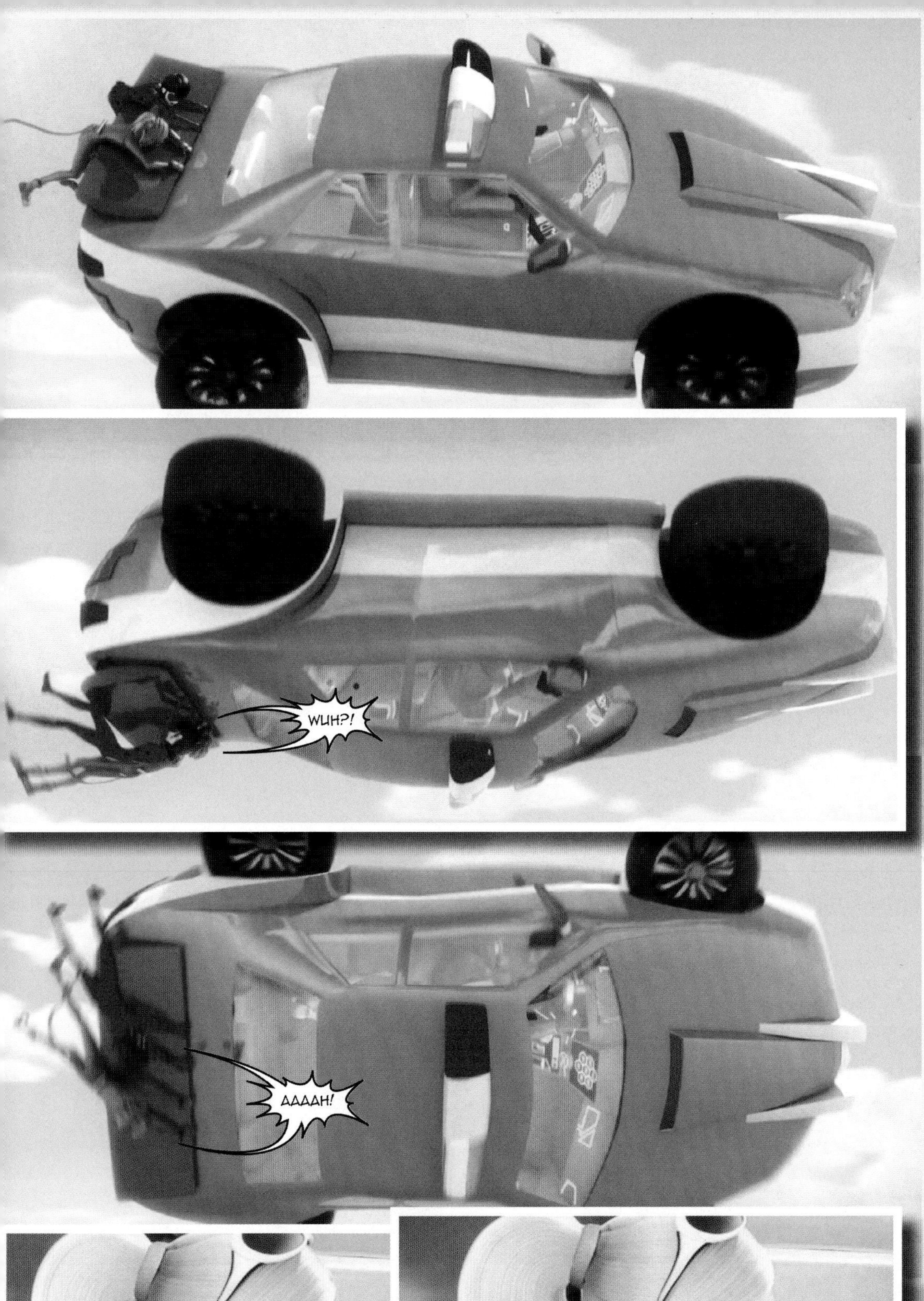
WUH?!
AAAAH!

SO, I KNOW THAT MARINETTE GIRL IS THE ONE WHO STOLE MY BRACELET.
SHE MUST BE ARRESTED!

HELLOOOO?!
AUTOPILOT ENGAGED.
ARE YOU LISTENING TO ME?
THANKS FOR THE LASSO, LASSIE!
SIGH
GASP

HEY!
WHERE ARE YOU GOING?! WHO'S GOING TO DRIVE THIS CAR?!?!
DID I EVER THANK YOU FOR THE LIFT?
HYAAAH!
POW!
STOMP
AHH!

OW!
GRAB ON TO ME!
NOOOO!
AAAAHHH!
LADYBUG!

BOOM!
WAAAH!

HUH?

WELL, HEY!

I'M HEAD OVER HEELS TO SEE YOU, M'LADY!

MMM-

OUCH!
YOU'RE WELCOME.

YOU OWE ME ONE!

SURE THING, BUT I'LL TAKE THE CREDIT FOR THAT!

MAYOR'S LIMOUSINE LOCATED.
THERE'S NO POINT RUNNING AFTER HIM ANYWAY. HE'S WAY OUT OF OUR REACH NOW!
WELL, IF IT'S THE MAYOR HE WANTS...
...HE'LL BE HEADING STRAIGHT FOR THE CITY HALL.
DO I SENSE A PLAN?!
HMPH!

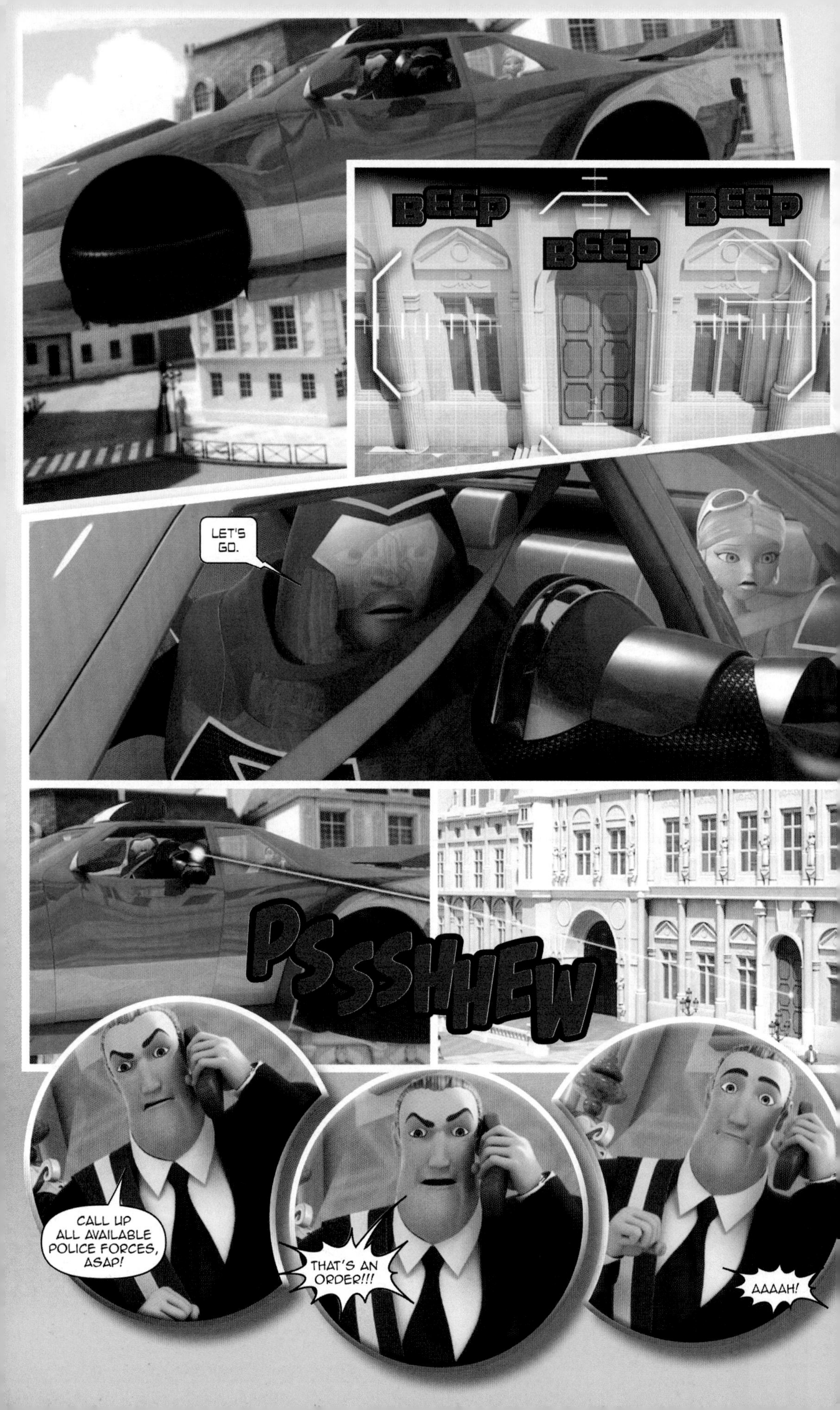
BEEP
BEEP
BEEP
LET'S GO.
PSSSHHEW
CALL UP ALL AVAILABLE POLICE FORCES, ASAP!
THAT'S AN ORDER!!!
AAAAH!

BOURGEOIS, I'M TAKING OVER. RELINQUISH YOUR POWERS!
NEVER!
PEW
PEW
GASP
THESE HANDCUFFS WON'T CHANGE MY MIND!
THEN MAYBE *THIS* WILL!

TWEET
HEY!
DADDY!
DON'T YOU DARE PUT A FINGER ON MY LITTLE GIRL...
SO MUCH FOR YOUR POWERS! HA HA, HA HA, HA HA!
PARIS HAS A NEW SUPER POWER: HIS NAME IS ROGERCOP.
I HEREBY RELINQUISH ALL AUTHORITY TO ROGERCOP.

ALL CITIZENS ARE ORDERED TO ANSWER TO HIM.
LADYBUG AND CAT NOIR ARE NOW OUTLAWS. THEY MUST BE HUNTED DOWN AND TAKEN INTO CUSTODY IMMEDIATELY!
GASP
GASP
UH-OH.

SO NOW WE'RE THE NATION'S MOST WANTED FELONS?!
WE HAVEN'T DONE ANYTHING!
EXACTLY!
YOU CAN'T ACCUSE SOMEONE WITHOUT PROOF! WE SHOULD GO AND DEFEND OURSELVES IN A COURT OF LAW!
NOT WHILE ROGERCOP'S THE CHIEF OF JUSTICE!
SIGH HOW MANY TIMES HAVE WE SAVED PARIS?
WE'RE **STILL** SAVING PARIS!

SOMETHING ABOUT PARIS...
...JUST MAKES YA WANNA DANCE!
WOULDN'T YOU AGREE?
ARREST HIM!
DOES THAT MEAN YOU WON'T BE JOINING ME?
HEH.
OOF!

YOU WON'T BE DANCING AFTER I'M THROUGH WITH YOU...
GASP
SHHH...
GO, LADYBUG, GO!
JUST GREAT...
LADYBUG...

...IT'S TIME
OR JUSTICE TO
PREVAIL.
PSSSHHEW
WHIR WHIR WHIR WHIR WHIR WHIR
YOU'VE GOT JUSTICE AND REVENGE ALL MIXED UP, ROGERCOP!
IT'S TIME FOR YOU TO SEE REAL JUSTICE!

LUCKY...
FWIP FWIP FWIP FWIP
...CHARM!
FWWSH

AN OVEN MITT? WHAT AM I SUPPOSED TO DO WITH THIS?!

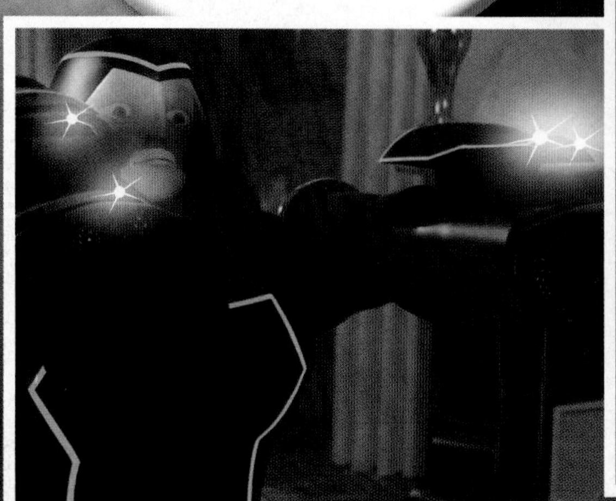

PEW
UGH!
PEW

PEW
PEW
PEW
PEW
PEW
PEW
PEW
PEW
PEW
FABULOUS... SO WRETCHEDLY FABULOUS!

UGH...
PEW
PEW
HEY, CHROME DOME!
WE'RE GOING TO SHORT CIRCUIT YOU, ROGERCOP!
TWEET

GET LADYBUG AND CAT NOIR!
AHHH!
AHHH!
GET 'EM OUT OF HERE!
HEY, MY HAIR!
PEW
PEW
PEW
STOP SHOOTING LIKE AN IDIOT, ROGERCOP! YOU'RE SUPPOSED TO SEIZE THEIR MIRACULOUSES!

WHENEVER YOU'RE READY, M'LADY!
DING!
DING!
DING!
DING!
DING!
OK, I HAVE AN IDEA, BUT I STILL NEED SOMETHING LIKE...
...A RING.

POW!

PEW
PEW
PEW

WHERE AM I GONNA GET A RING FROM?!
PEW
PEW
PEW

I MIGHT JUST BE ABLE TO HELP WITH THAT...

LADYBUG, OVER THERE!
THAT'S CHLOÉ'S BRACELET... EXACTLY WHAT I NEED!
FWIP
FEND OFF ROGERCOP AS LONG AS YOU CAN!
WHENEVER YOU'RE READY!
CATACLYSM!
CRUNCH!

PEW
PEW
PEW
SCREEECH
CRACKLE
PEW
PEW
CRASH!
URGH...

PEW
PEW
I GOTCHA!
#@&!!*¥$%£??
NOOOOO!
CRACK!
CLICK
NO MORE EVIL DOING FOR YOU, LITTLE AKUMA!

TIME TO DE-EVILIZE!
FWWSH
HO HO HO!
FWOOSH
AHA!
FWWSH
POLICE
WHAT AM I DOING UP HERE?
POUND IT!

AS ROGERCOP WOULD SAY, "JUSTICE HAS PREVAILED IN THE STREETS OF PARIS!"
POLICE
BEEP
BEEP
BEEP
I'D STICK AROUND BUT THEN YOU'D SEE ME WITHOUT MY MASK AND... YOU WOULDN'T BE ABLE TO RESIST ME!
HA HA... I DOUBT THAT, BUT I'LL HAVE TO TAKE YOUR WORD FOR IT.
HMPH!
YOU MAY HAVE ELUDED ME THIS TIME, LADYBUG, BUT ONE OF THESE DAYS, I'LL BE RULING THE WORLD.
AND YOU AND CAT NOIR WON'T BE A PART OF IT!

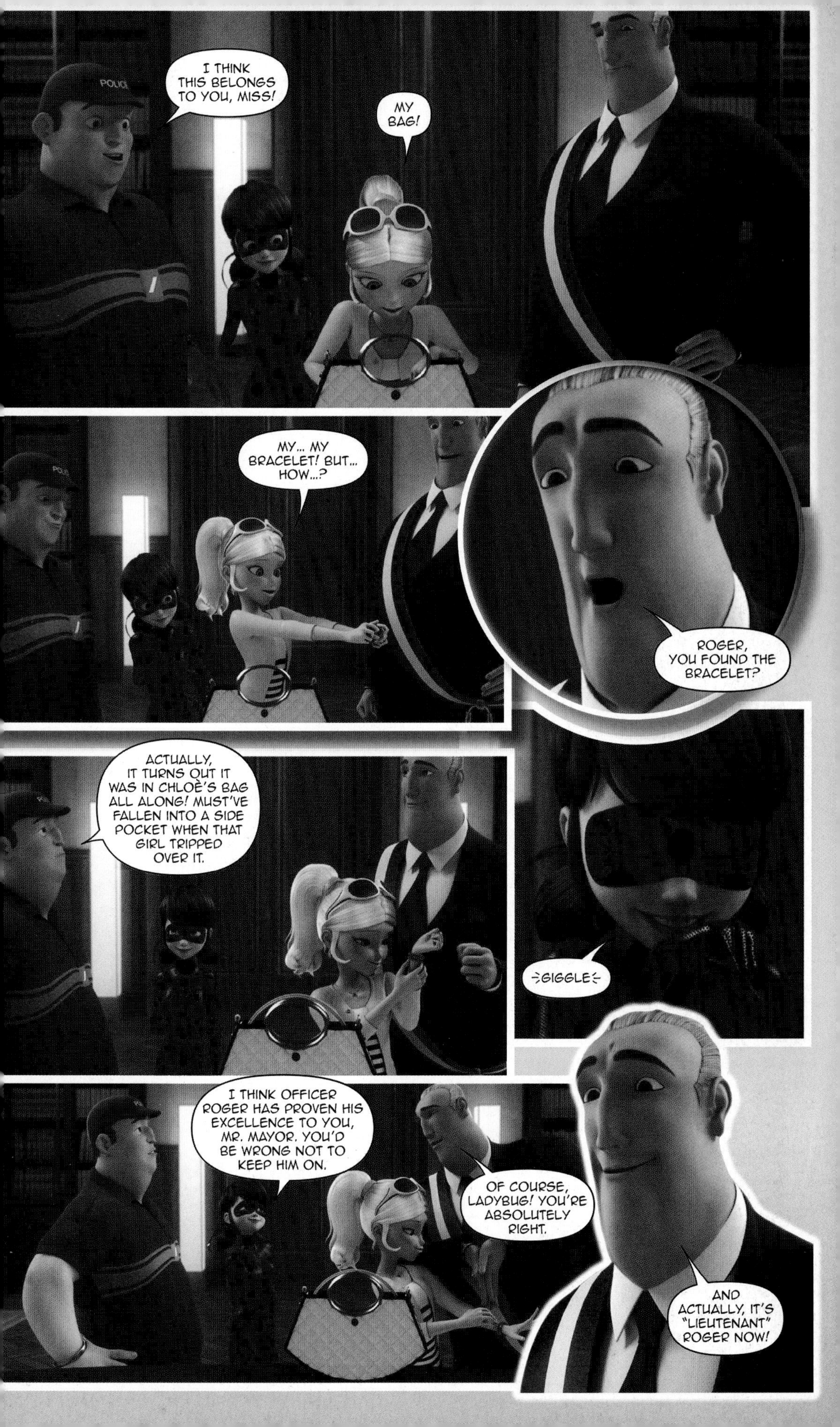
I THINK THIS BELONGS TO YOU, MISS!
MY BAG!
MY... MY BRACELET! BUT... HOW...?
ROGER, YOU FOUND THE BRACELET?
ACTUALLY, IT TURNS OUT IT WAS IN CHLOÈ'S BAG ALL ALONG! MUST'VE FALLEN INTO A SIDE POCKET WHEN THAT GIRL TRIPPED OVER IT.
GIGGLE
I THINK OFFICER ROGER HAS PROVEN HIS EXCELLENCE TO YOU, MR. MAYOR. YOU'D BE WRONG NOT TO KEEP HIM ON.
OF COURSE, LADYBUG! YOU'RE ABSOLUTELY RIGHT.
AND ACTUALLY, IT'S "LIEUTENANT" ROGER NOW!

THANK YOU, MR. MAYOR!
I'M PROUD TO BE ON THE FORCE, AND I VOW TO UPHOLD MY FIRM BELIEF THAT EVERY CITIZEN IS INNOCENT UNTIL PROVEN GUILTY!
BEEP BEEP
VERY GOOD, A VALUABLE LESSON LEARNED. RIGHT, CHLOÉ?
UGH! YES, DADDY!
LESSON LEARNED.